Hello Kitty's
Superterrific Sleepover!

by Mark McVeigh
Illustrated by Sachiho Hino

SCHOLASTIC INC.

All rights reserved. Published by Scholastic Inc., *Publishers since 1920.* SCHOLASTIC and associated logos are trademarks and/or registered trademarks of Scholastic Inc.

The publisher does not have any control over and does not assume any responsibility for author or third-party websites or their content.

This book is a work of fiction. Names, characters, places, and incidents are either the product of the author's imagination or are used fictitiously, and any resemblance to actual persons, living or dead, business establishments, events, or locales is entirely coincidental.

ISBN 978-1-338-11363-1

10 9 8 7 6 5 4 3 2 1   17 18 19 20 21

Printed in the U.S.A.   40

First printing 2017
Book design by Angela Jun

Hello Kitty, Mimmy, and Mama were
in the kitchen.
Something smelled delicious!

Tonight was Hello Kitty and

Mimmy's sleepover.

They were busy making cupcakes.

Then they put candy in bowls,

drinks on ice, and flowers in pretty vases.

Fifi was coming over any minute.

Ring, ring — was that the doorbell?

No, it was the oven.

The cupcakes were done.

Mimmy frosted them carefully.

Then Mama would decorate them.

Ring, ring!

This time it was the doorbell.

It was Fifi.

She was in her pajamas.

Hello Kitty and Mimmy took their friend

to the playroom.

First, they played pin-the-tail-on-the-donkey.
Fifi put a blindfold on Hello Kitty.

Hello Kitty got a little dizzy spinning around.

Everyone was having a great time!

There were lots of toys in the playroom.

Hello Kitty played with toys.

Fifi and Mimmy played a board game.

It was almost time for dinner.

Everyone was hungry.

So they all went to the kitchen.

The pizza had arrived.

Everyone was happy.

Hello Kitty and Mimmy passed out
the slices of pizza.

Everyone had more than one slice.

The pizza was super yummy!

Then everyone helped clean up.

Hello Kitty and Fifi washed the dishes.

Mimmy put everything away.

Soon they all went back to the playroom.

Mimmy brought the cupcakes with her.

Should they eat the cupcakes?

They decided to tell spooky stories first.

Fifi started her story in a quiet voice.

They both leaned closer.

Then the lights went out!

What happened?

They stayed close together.

Hello Kitty turned the lights on.

Everyone was fine.

Oh, no! The cupcakes were missing!

Hello Kitty, Mimmy, and Fifi
looked everywhere for the cupcakes.
But they couldn't find them anywhere.

They went to the kitchen to ask Mama.
They were surprised—Mama had the
cupcakes!

Mama had forgotten to put on the sprinkles.
That's why she turned off the lights and
took them.
It also made Fifi's story spookier.

Hello Kitty and the friends giggled.

The mystery was solved!

Everyone ate tasty cupcakes while Fifi

finished her scary story.

It was almost time for bed.

It was the best sleepover ever!